THE TWELVE DANCING PRINCESSES

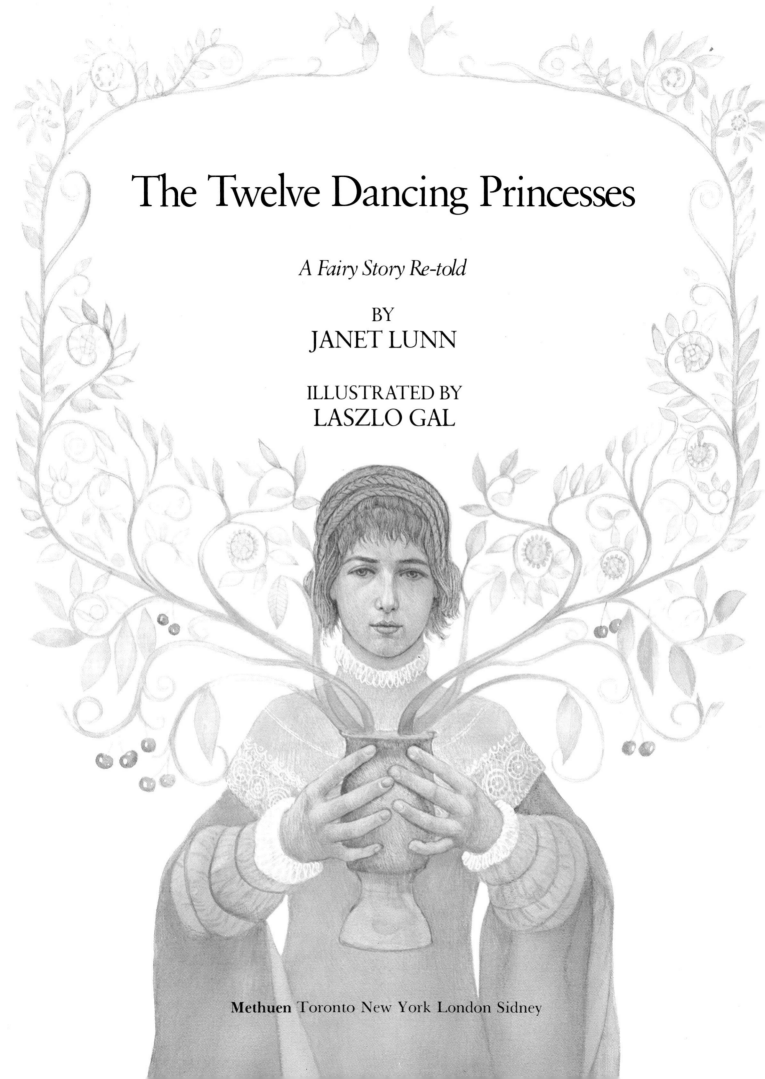

The Twelve Dancing Princesses

A Fairy Story Re-told

BY
JANET LUNN

ILLUSTRATED BY
LASZLO GAL

Methuen Toronto New York London Sidney

To my sister Zimmie because we loved this story together when we were small.
JL

To my daughters Raffaella and Marika with all my love.
LG

NCE UPON A TIME
in a faraway place there lived a simple farm boy. He lived alone, with no one to care for him, and he earned what little he had hoeing turnips and cabbages. In his spare time he grew roses and columbines which he sold in town on market day.

One night on his way home from market the boy stopped in a little wood beside a brook. He tethered his horse and, after sharing his supper of bread and cheese with the birds and the squirrels, he lay down to rest on a soft bed of moss. He fell at once into a deep sleep and dreamed he saw a golden palace. In front of the palace stood twelve rose bushes all in a row. One of the rose bushes leaned toward him as though blown by a gust of wind, and it spoke to him, saying, "Travel west along the rainbow, west and west again, and if you are steadfast and true you will find your heart's desire." As the dream faded, he saw the twelve rose bushes change into twelve princesses more beautiful than the morning sun.

The boy awoke. Straightway he made up his mind that he would find the golden palace. The sky was still dark and owls and whippoorwills were still hooting and calling when he set forth on his journey. West he went and ever west over mountains, along valleys and across wide rivers, and every time he lost his way a rainbow arched across the sky to lead him.

At the bright edge of a dark forest, the boy came upon an old woman chasing a pig. He caught the little pig by its quick and curly tail and dropped it wriggling and squirming into its pen.

"You have done me a kindness," the old woman said. "In return I will grant you one wish."

"I wish to find the palace of the twelve princesses," said the boy.

"Then listen carefully to me," the old woman answered, "for first there are things you must know." And they sat down together on a bench beside her cottage door.

"The land you seek is on the far side of this deep forest," she began. "It lies under a strange spell. It is a bleak and sorrowful place. Nothing grows there.

"It was not always so. Once it was the fairest land in all the world where the king was wise and just and his twelve daughters brought happiness to every heart. In the royal gardens fountains splashed joyously in the summer sun and froze in graceful arches under the winter moon. Bluebirds and finches and golden orioles sang in the trees. Roses bloomed everywhere. Mazes of cedar and pine hid in their dark paths secrets only the king's daughters knew.

"In those gardens the twelve princesses grew to be so beautiful that the sun and the stars drew closer to the earth just to look at them. Kings and princes came from near and far to beg to be their husbands. They brought presents of rare spices, perfume and fine cloth. The king was very pleased.

"But the princesses would have nothing to do with any of them. They had become as vain as they were beautiful. They kept to their own rooms and refused to go out into the royal gardens. And when they no longer walked in the gardens, the birds stopped singing and the roses began to fade.

"When the people learned that the roses were dying they brought a petition to the princesses to beg them not to hide themselves away, for it was an ancient belief that the kingdom would prosper only as long as the royal gardens bloomed. But the princesses paid no attention. They cared for no one but themselves. They grew silent and secretive.

"One day their lady-in-waiting brought word to the king of an odd state of affairs. That morning the shoes that stood beside each princess's bed were so worn and full of holes they looked as if they'd been danced in all night. The king sent for his youngest daughter to question her because, although the eldest is the most beautiful, the king had always loved this gentle-hearted girl the best.

"'I cannot say,' she answered gravely to all his questions. And the king was very angry.

"That night the king locked his daughters in their bedchamber. But the next morning a pair of ragged dancing shoes stood beside each bed. And the following morning it was the same . . . and every morning after.

"While the princesses kept the royal shoemakers busy making new shoes, the king sent his pages, his soldiers, his wise men and his fool to search the princesses' rooms. Not a clue was found. He sent spies to look through the windows, but the girls pulled their curtains against the prying eyes. He had three sets of stout oak doors built over the entrance to their apartments, and he put watchmen to guard them. But the worn-out dancing shoes were still there each morning. And still no one knew where the princesses danced each night.

"The king sent out a proclamation:

Hear Ye! Hear Ye!

The man who discovers the secret of the dancing shoes shall gain the hand of my fairest daughter in marriage, and at my death he shall inherit my kingdom. Three days and three nights shall any man have who dares to try. But the man who fails shall lose his head.

"First came a fine prince. The king entertained him splendidly all day. That evening the prince was given a large chair to sit in just outside the princesses' bedchamber, and their door was left open so that he could find out where they went at night. But the princesses brought him cake and wine and soon he was fast asleep.

When morning came the new shoes were as worn out and as full of holes as ever. On the second and third nights the same thing happened, and the king ordered the prince's head to be cut off. Others came after him — some say dozens, some say hundreds. They all lost their heads, and the secret of the dancing shoes stayed safe in the keeping of the princesses. And so things are to this day."

The old woman got up. She went into her cottage and brought out an old russet velvet cloak. "If you would discover the secret and win the kingdom, take this cloak," she said. "It will make you invisible. But beware, for the youngest princess, though gentle in her ways, is wary as a squirrel and quick as a chipmunk and cannot easily be deceived. Above all, heed well these three warnings for your life will depend on them.

"The first is this:

Nothing must you drink or eat,
Once the night's dark shadows meet.

"The second is this:

Reveal not face or finger tip,
Nor suffer sound to pass your lip.

"And the third is this:

Stay not past dawn's discovering hand,
Or forever stay within that land."

The boy thanked the old woman. He stowed the cloak carefully in his bag and, whistling, rode off through the forest. On he rode through a gray and dreary land, and at last he came to the golden palace where he soon found himself in the presence of the king.

The king looked with disdain on the boy's dusty hat, his patched and threadbare clothes and his heavy country boots.

"Well?" he asked.

The boy bowed deeply and said, "Your Majesty, I have come to beg the position of gardener's boy in the royal gardens and to solve the riddle of the dancing shoes. May it please your Majesty, I am said to have a way with both riddles and roses."

"Riddles!" growled the king. "Do you realize, simpleton, that hundreds of royal princes have already failed to solve this puzzle? Of course I must let you try," he added coldly. "But understand – if you can – that in three days you will certainly lose your head."

So it was, as the shadows of night gathered softly around his feet, that the boy was seated in the big chair just outside the princesses' bedchamber. Before long the princesses came to give him cake and wine, and he saw that they were as beautiful as in his dream. He thanked them courteously, but he had not forgotten the old woman's warning:

Nothing must you drink or eat,
Once the night's dark shadows meet.

And when they had gone, he crumbled the cake and pushed it through a crack in the floor for the mice to feed on, and he poured the wine down after it. "There's a party for you, little friends," he murmured. Then he pulled his hat down over his eyes and began to snore loudly.

The moment the princesses heard his snores, they were up out of their beds. They rushed to their wardrobes and pulled out their silk and velvet gowns. As they dressed, they chattered in excited whispers – all but the youngest. "Sisters," she said in a low voice, "I fear something is wrong."

"Foolish girl" – they laughed – "Stay with the gardener's boy if you like."

Swiftly they thrust their feet into their new dancing shoes, then turned as one to the mirrored wall at the end of the room and said,

Open wall and let us through,
You called to us, we come to you.

Slowly the wall opened. One by one the princesses lifted their delicate skirts and started down a stone stairway.

The boy had been listening to their talk and the rustling of their silks. Throwing the cloak of invisibility around him he strode across the room, and was down the stairs after them so fast that he trod on the hem of the youngest princess's gown.

"Oh, sisters," she cried, "someone has stepped on my gown!"

"Oh, half-wit! You've stepped on it yourself," said the eldest, and she led the way down the dark stairway. Down and down they went until the stairs became a pale lawn that crackled and shimmered like needles of fine glass in the twilight. All around were silver trees, their branches gleaming as though sheathed in ice.

The boy gazed about him in wonder. By the time he had gathered his wits the princesses were nowhere in sight. Quickly he reached up and broke a tiny branch from the nearest tree. It broke with a sharp sound like glass cracking, and he heard the youngest princess cry out, "Oh sisters, did you hear the noise?"

"Whatever is wrong with you tonight?" snapped the eldest. The boy hid the shining twig in his pocket and followed them.

Soon he came to a second wood where the trees were all of gold. He broke off a golden twig, and the noise it made was like a tree falling.

"Oh sisters," the youngest cried out. Her sisters hushed her, and their voices led him to a third wood where the trees were all of diamonds and emerald leaves and fruits of sapphire and ruby. No breeze stirred, but the light from the jewels glittered and danced among the leaves, and it seemed to the boy that magic lived in every branch.

He broke off a diamond twig and picked a ruby cherry – the sounds were like crashing thunder. The youngest princess cried out and her sisters called her foolish. The boy heard and followed.

He came at last to the edge of the wood, to pearl white sands and a round lake, deep and black and still. From the middle of the lake there rose an alabaster castle, that seemed to gather to its glowing surface all the pale white light that was everywhere in the underground world.

The twelve princesses were already pulling away from the shore in twelve little glass boats rowed by twelve princes. The boy watched unhappily from the edge of the wood. Then he sat down by the silent water to wait.

Just before dawn the boats came gliding across the lake. The boy raced back through the woods and was snoring in his chair when the princesses came to see if he had moved.

In the morning, in a far corner of the gardens, he took the silver and gold and diamond twigs from his pocket. To his horror he saw that he held in his hand three ordinary dried-up old sticks. And the ruby was as black and wizened as any garden cherry left on the tree to be buffeted about by the winter wind.

"Now I'll lose my head for sure," groaned the boy. He stuffed the useless sticks back in his pocket and set to work watering and weeding. Then he began to sing to cheer himself up.

He sang so loudly that the princesses came out of their rooms to find out what had made him so merry. Not one of them spoke to him as they sailed by along the path, but the youngest princess reached out and touched the rose bush he was pruning and the boy thought it grew green at her touch.

That night, just as before, the princesses gave the boy cake and wine. Just as before he pretended to sleep, and the princesses, as fast as children playing hide and seek, slipped into their ball gowns and hurried down into their underground world.

This time the boy raced after them and settled himself behind the prince in the bow of the youngest princess's boat.

"How hard the rowing is tonight," sighed the prince. The princess said it was surely the heat, but her face was troubled and she shivered.

As they approached the castle the sound of music floated over the water toward them – music so lilting, so inviting, no feet could resist its magic. Laughing and singing, they danced their way up into the castle, through great halls and down a wide curved staircase into a huge ballroom. The floor was made of black marble that reflected from its depths a thousand lighted candles. The walls were hung with rich tapestries, and at one end of the room was a banquet table set with a sumptuous feast. In a high gallery musicians played, and their strange, wild music swirled through the hall like the light through the diamond trees.

All night the princesses danced and feasted and drank sweet wine, while the boy stood back among the shadows and watched. The youngest princess turned her eyes often and uneasily toward the place where he stood, and more than once she stumbled as she danced. The boy longed to take off the cloak of invisibility for one moment to show her it was only the gardener's boy but – just in time – he remembered the old woman's words:

Reveal not face or finger tip,
Nor suffer sound to pass your lip.

So he moved in and out among the shadows to keep her from being frightened, and on the way back across the lake he sat in the eldest princess's boat. She was not in the least upset when the prince complained of the weight. "What a lazy fellow you are," was all she said and yawned sleepily.

As soon as the boat touched the shore the boy jumped out. He ran on ahead and was snoring away when the princesses came to make sure he was sleeping.

The next morning he discovered that the rose bush the princess had touched had three new shoots. He whistled loudly and the princesses, filled with curiosity, came to see what had happened.

They strolled past as they had done the day before – all but the youngest who stopped to admire the new shoots.

The boy picked the greenest one and gave it to her, bowing.

"Your Highness, perhaps you might like this rose slip even more than silver or gold or precious jewels," he said.

The princess turned pale. Her eyes grew wide with alarm but she said nothing and hurried after her sisters.

That night the princesses' gowns were finer than silken spiders' webs. Their faces were alight with an unearthly gaiety, and when they danced their feet were as nimble as hummingbirds' wings. That night there was an excitement in the air that drew the boy out of the shadows, and the music was so enticing that when the princesses danced, he danced behind each one in turn, too. When they feasted he stood behind each chair. But he kept in mind the old woman's words, and he touched neither wine nor food. And as the night began to fade, he remembered her final warning:

Stay not past dawn's discovering hand,
Or forever stay within that land.

He snatched the golden wine goblet from the hand of the youngest princess and, hiding it under his cloak, he ran from the castle.

Back in his chair, with his eyes tightly shut, the boy heard the eldest princess say scornfully, "So much for your fears! You see, he sleeps more soundly than all the others. He is ugly and stupid and won't even notice his head has gone."

The princesses sighed with relief, but as the last one turned away the boy felt a tear fall on his cheek.

He waited anxiously for daylight, but when he looked at the golden goblet in the morning sun it had become as rusty as a tin cup buried for a hundred years in the earth. He was heart-sick.

"What good are magic cloaks and wise warnings," he said sadly. "What have I got to show the king but old dead sticks." All the same, when the king sent for him he went bravely and told his tale just as it had happened.

The princesses said nothing. The king laughed.

"So!" he sneered, more scornfully than the eldest princess had ever sneered. "And have you, by any chance, brought me these treasures from my daughters' underground kingdom?"

One by one the boy put the dried-up sticks and the black and wizened cherry into the rusty goblet. As he slowly handed the goblet to the king, the youngest princess reached out and dropped the rose slip into it.

Before their eyes the goblet changed into gold. The twigs became silver and gold and diamond. The cherry was a sparkling ruby. Only the little green rose slip resting brightly on top was unchanged.

No one was more astonished than the boy, not even the king who stared and stared, and at last, as if in a dream, put out his hand for the golden goblet from the alabaster castle.

"You have won," he declared. "You shall have the hand of my fairest daughter in marriage, and when I die you shall inherit my kingdom together."

The boy looked shyly at the youngest princess. "Will you marry me?" he asked. "Yes, I will," she said.

At once the spell was broken. The gardens burst into flower and the birds began to sing. The land was green again and the people danced in the streets. The youngest princess married the gardener's boy and, in time, her eleven sisters chose husbands for themselves and went off to live in faraway places.

Years later when the old king died and it came time for the gardener's boy and the youngest princess to be king and queen, they ruled the kingdom well, being both wise and full of wit. And happiness reigned all the years of their lives.

Published in the United States by Methuen, Inc.,
733 Third Avenue, New York 10017

Published in Australia by Methuen of Australia
Pty. Ltd., 301 Kent Street, Sydney.
ISBN 0-458-93890-4

DESIGN: *Brant Cowie/Artplus*
Printed in Canada

1 2 3 4 5   3 2 1 0 9

Canadian Cataloguing in Publication Data

Lunn, Janet, 1928-
  The twelve dancing princesses.

Based on the story Die zertanzten Schuhe by the
Brothers Grimm.

ISBN 0-458-93890-4

I. Gal, Laszlo. II. Grimm, Jakob, 1785-1863. Die
zertanzten Schuhe. III. Title.

PS8573.U55T94   jC813'.5'4   C79-094770-6
PZ8.L85Tw

Library of Congress Cataloguing in Publication Data

Lunn, Janet Louise Swoboda, 1928-
  The twelve dancing princesses.

  Based on Die zertanzten Schuhe by J. L. K. Grimm.
  SUMMARY: A retelling of the tale of 12 princesses
who dance secretly all night long and the soldier who
follows them and discovers where they dance.
  [1. Fairy tales. 2. Folklore—Germany] I. Gal,
Laszlo. II. Grimm, Jakob Ludwig Karl, 1785-1863. Die
zertanzten Schuhe. III. Title.
PZ8.L976Tw   398.2'1'0943   [E]   79-19739
ISBN 0-416-30601-2